God Gave Us Heaven

by Lisa Tawn Bergren • art by Laura J. Bryant

WATERBROOK
PRESS

GOD GAVE US HEAVEN

Hardcover ISBN 978-1-4000-7446-4
eBook ISBN 978-0-307-73086-2

Copyright © 2008 by Lisa Tawn Bergren
Illustrations © 2008 by Laura Bryant; www.laurabryant.com

Published in the United States by WaterBrook, an imprint of the Crown Publishing Group, a division of Penguin Random House LLC, New York.

WATERBROOK® and its deer colophon are registered trademarks of Penguin Random House LLC.

Library of Congress Cataloging-in-Publication Data.
Bergren, Lisa Tawn.
    God gave us heaven / by Lisa Tawn Bergren ; illustrated by Laura Bryant.
      p. cm.
    ISBN 978-1-4000-7446-4
    [1. Heaven—Fiction. 2. Christian life—Fiction. 3. Polar bear—Fiction. 4. Bears—Fiction.]
    I. Bryant, Laura J., ill. II. Title
      PZ7.B452233Goh 2009
      [E]—dc22
                                                    2009004095

Printed in the United States of America
2020

16

For all those who already know
the wonders of heaven, but in particular,

Mady Grace, 1996–2002

"Papa, what's heav'n?"

"Why, heaven is God's home…
the most amazing place we'll ever get to see."

"More amazing than Glacier Bay?" Little Cub asked.
"Glacier Bay is the best place ever."

"Yes, Little Cub. Even better than Glacier Bay."

"God has great plans for you, Little Cub."

"For me?"

"For you. Both here, and later, when we get to heaven.
God loves us and never wants to be far from us. He's made
a way for us to be with him forever, in heaven."

"When do we get to see heaven, Papa?"

"When our life here is over."

"When we die?"

"Yes, Little Cub, when we die."

"Will I be old like Grandma when I go to heaven?"

"I hope so, Little Cub. I hope you get to live a long and full life before you see heaven. But some of us get to see it sooner than others."

"They do? How come?"

"They get sick or something bad happens. But the good news is that no matter what bad things happen here, nothing bad happens in heaven!"

"Nothing bad at all?"

"No more tears, no more sadness, no more pain.
Only good. Only smiles!"

Little Cub thought on that for a while. "Will we eat in heaven?"

"Will we eat? Will we eat! We'll have more food than we need! It'll be the best of all polar bear feasts!"

"Every day?"

"Every single day."

"What else will we do in heaven?"

"Worship God and explore the best place we've ever seen."

"Will we get bored of that?"

"I doubt it. Heaven will be a million times better than even this!"

"Can we take our stuff to heaven?"

"No, we won't need our stuff there, Little Cub." He paused and lifted her backpack from her shoulders. "Feel how heavy that is? Doesn't it feel good to have it off of you?"

Little Cub nodded.

"Sometimes we think we need stuff, but it's just more weight for us to carry. Our best stuff doesn't weigh anything at all—stuff like love,

family,

friends,

and faith.

That's where our real blessings are."

"What will God look like, Papa?"

"Hmm…you know what Mama looks like?
How she looks like love to us?
God will be like that…"

"'Cept a hundred times better!"

"Exactly."

"Will we be angels?"

"No. Only angels are angels. God made us polar bears for a reason."

"Shoot. I wanted to fly."

Papa laughed. "Me too. But you never know what we'll get to do in heaven. I bet we'll think it's even better than flying."

"Will I get to see you in heaven?"

"I think so, Little Cub. I think we'll see all our loved ones there. It will be like the best family reunion ever."

"How do we get there, Papa? To heaven, I mean."

"Hmm… Let's say this side of the canyon is life here, on earth.
And that side over there—where we find the path home—is heaven.

God knew that our bad choices might keep us from him forever. Might even wash us away! He didn't want that. He loves us too much."

"So he sent his very own Son, Jesus, to be our bridge. All we have to do is walk across it to head toward our forever home."

Little Cub thought on that. "I like Jesus," she said.

"So do I, Little Cub. So do I."

"Will I have a room in heaven?"

"Oh yes, there will be many rooms
in heaven."

"Will it be as cozy as mine?"

"The coziest ever,
Little Cub."

"Will I sleep in heaven?" she said with a yawn.
It had been a very big day. Papa yawned too and they
giggled together.

"Heaven will be full of all the things we love most,"
Papa said. "And right now, sleep sounds heavenly to me."

Little Cub went to sleep and dreamed of seeing
God and his angels, of singing and smiling
all day long. Of her best friends
and her whole family being
with her forever.
Of playing,
of laughing,
of everything good.

And she was glad, so glad, that
God had given them all
heaven.

Enjoy the rest of the God Gave Us series!

Available in eBook:

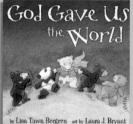

Available in Print:

Available as Board Book: